THIS

BOOK

BELONGS

TO _____

Disney's
SMALL WORLD LIBRARY
THE MAGIC OF MUSIC
An Adventure in Spain

GROLIER ENTERPRISES INC.
DANBURY, CONNECTICUT

ISBN: 0-7172-8231-7

"Welcome to Spain!" Professor Costas called to Mickey and Minnie. Professor Costas taught music at the University of Granada in southern Spain. Mickey and Minnie were attending the Festival of Music and Dance taking place in Granada and writing a magazine article about music in Spain. They were staying at Professor Costas's house during the visit.

"I am so happy to see you, my friends!" Professor Costas said warmly, leading Mickey and Minnie into a shady courtyard.

"We're looking forward to bringing back a great story for our magazine," Mickey said.

"I only wish I could show you around the city myself," said Professor Costas, "but I will be busy helping my chorus practice for the concert. However," he said with a twinkle in his eye, "I do have a special surprise for you."

Mickey and Minnie followed Professor Costas to a small corral surrounded by a wooden fence. The professor said proudly, "Meet Panchito and Panchita. They will take you around Granada in style!"

Two little donkeys stared back at Mickey and Minnie. "I've never ridden a donkey before," Minnie said, snapping photos of the animals, "but it sure sounds like fun!"

"I must warn you. Like all donkeys, my little friends can be stubborn," Professor Costas said. "They sometimes have their own ideas of the best road to travel. However, after living with me, Panchito and Panchita have become music lovers. If you have trouble getting them to move, just sing them a song."

The next morning, Mickey and Minnie followed
Professor Costas back to the corral.

Once they were settled in their saddles, Mickey cried,
"Giddyap, Panchito!" But the little donkey just stood there
munching hay. Minnie giggled.

"Don't forget—they like music!" Professor Costas said.

Minnie hummed a happy tune, and the donkeys took
off at a trot!

Mickey and Minnie nearly bounced out of their saddles at first.

"Stop! Whoa!" cried Mickey as the donkeys trotted away from the city. "We're headed the wrong way!"

But Panchito and Panchita just kept trotting away from the city up into the green hills.

"Where are they taking us?" Mickey wondered.

Minnie cupped her hand to her ear. "Listen!" she said.

Mickey heard a beautiful voice coming from nearby.

The donkeys' long ears twitched. They trotted over the hill and stopped in front of a shepherdess who was singing to her flock of sheep. When the girl saw Mickey and Minnie, she stopped singing.

"Your voice is beautiful," Mickey said after he introduced himself and Minnie.

The shepherdess smiled shyly and said her name was Carmen. "It may seem strange, but the sheep like it when I sing," she told them. "My voice teacher is training me to sing opera—so I like to practice here with my sheep. I hope someday I will be good enough to perform in the music festival in Granada."

"We're going to the festival tomorrow," Minnie told
Carmen.

She explained their assignment for the magazine.

" 'Shepherdess Sings Opera to Sheep!' " Mickey said.
"This can be part of our story."

While Minnie snapped pictures of Carmen and her
flock, the shepherdess told Mickey about her family's life
in Granada. For many years, they had tended sheep and
grown olives in the rich soil.

"Oh no!" Mickey suddenly cried.

He pointed to Panchito and Panchita trotting over a
nearby hill. "Where are they going now?" he asked.

Minnie looked in the direction Mickey was pointing. "I
don't know, but we'd better find out!" she said.

Mickey and Minnie thanked Carmen and said a hasty
good-bye. Then they ran off after the two donkeys.

When they reached Panchito and Panchita, Mickey and Minnie tried to point them toward the city. Once again, the donkeys had their own ideas about where to go next. Mickey tried singing the song that Carmen had been singing, but the donkeys paid no attention to him.

"I think they hear something else," Minnie said.

Mickey and Minnie both listened. They could just make out the gentle strumming of a guitar.

"The donkeys have led us to one new friend already," Mickey said. "We might as well follow them this time."

The donkeys carried Mickey and Minnie up to the garden of a beautiful white-walled palace. Mickey thumbed through his guidebook. "This must be the Generalife," he said. "It was once the country home of the Spanish rulers."

"I've never seen such a pretty place," said Minnie.
"It's like walking into the pages of a fairy tale." From atop
the green hill, Mickey and Minnie could see the snow-
covered Sierra Nevada mountains.

Panchito and Panchita kept trotting along. They finally
stopped next to a young man playing a guitar.

The young man looked up when he heard the donkeys approach.

"I'm sorry," Mickey said, sliding off Panchito's back. "We didn't mean to startle you. We just stopped to hear your music."

Mickey and Minnie introduced themselves to the young man, whose name was Tomás.

"You play the guitar very well," said Minnie.

"Thank you," said Tomás. "My family makes guitars here in Granada, and I have been playing since I was a little boy. I'll be playing at the festival tomorrow night."

Mickey explained that he and Minnie were writing a story about Spanish music for a magazine. Minnie photographed Tomás while he played his guitar.

"We'll be sure to come see you at the festival tomorrow," said Mickey.

Then Mickey and Minnie hopped back on their donkeys. After saying good-bye, Minnie hummed a few bars of Tomás's tune, and the donkeys headed toward Granada.

Before long, Panchito and Panchita turned off the main road and started trotting toward a little village.

"Whoa!" cried Mickey. "Not again!"

Minnie tried singing, but the donkeys were determined to go their own way.

Mickey sighed. "There's no stopping them, anyway," he said.

Soon the donkeys came to a stop in front of a small white-walled restaurant. Through the open windows, Mickey and Minnie could hear guitar music, stamping feet, and loud cheering.

"Let's see what's going on," said Minnie. "It sounds like there's quite a party going on inside."

Mickey tied Panchito and Panchita to a tree outside the restaurant.

Inside the restaurant, a flamenco guitarist and dancer entertained a crowd of tourists who were eating, singing, and clapping. A waitress led Mickey and Minnie to a table. She recommended some Spanish favorites—a cold soup of chopped vegetables called *gazpacho*, and a steaming plate of yellow rice with seafood and chicken called *paella*.

Minnie snapped pictures of the dancers, as the sounds of the lively music and stamping feet shook the floor of the restaurant.

As soon as they were finished with their delicious meal, Mickey and Minnie approached the dancer. She told them her name was Lucía.

"Your dress is beautiful!" Minnie said, admiring Lucía's colorful costume. "And so is your dancing."

"Flamenco dancing is even more fun with a partner. Here, let me show you," Lucía said as she grabbed Mickey's hand. "Come dance!" she cried. Lucía stamped her feet and gestured for Mickey to do the same.

Minnie laughed as she photographed Mickey's attempts at flamenco dancing. But soon Mickey and Lucía pulled her onto the stage as well.

Minnie was swept up by the loud strumming of the guitar and the cheering of the crowd. She and Mickey stamped their feet and clapped their hands.

"Shouldn't you be taking notes?" Minnie asked Mickey breathlessly.

"Don't worry," Mickey said. "I'll never forget a moment of this!"

After the song ended, Mickey and Minnie thanked Lucía for the lesson.

"I'm so glad to have met you," Lucía said. "Flamenco music always brings people together.

"I am going to dance in the festival tomorrow night,"
Lucía continued. "Would you like to be my guests
backstage?"

"That would be wonderful!" Mickey and Minnie said.

Then the friends said good-bye, and Mickey and
Minnie left the little restaurant to head home. This time
Panchito and Panchita were ready to go home, too.

Soon the two tired donkeys turned up the little path to
Professor Costas's house.

"Welcome home, my friends!" Professor Costas called. "Tell me about your day."

Mickey and Minnie told him about all the new friends they had met, and about being invited backstage for the festival.

The next evening Mickey and Minnie left for the festival with Professor Costas. In the lobby they met Carmen and Tomás. Then Mickey and Minnie slipped backstage to see Lucía. When they finally found her, she looked very upset.

"My partner sprained his ankle," she explained, "and I can't dance without a partner." Suddenly her face brightened. "What about you?" she asked Mickey hopefully. "Will you dance with me tonight?"

Before Mickey had a chance to answer, Minnie and Lucía whisked him off to the dressing room to get a costume.

"But I haven't practiced enough to be in the show!" Mickey cried.

"Don't worry," Lucía said. "You were wonderful yesterday. Just listen to the music."

The big curtain rose. Mickey, Minnie, and Lucía
watched the musicians and dancers perform. Then, as the
flamenco music started, Lucía and Mickey began to
dance.

"You're doing great!" Lucía whispered to Mickey as
she stamped her feet.

And the audience thought so, too. When the dance
was over, everyone stood up and clapped.

"Bravo!" cried Minnie when Mickey and Lucía returned backstage.

Just then a young man with a pad of paper and a camera pushed through the performers. "Excuse me," he said. "But I'm reporting on the festival. Can you share any thoughts about music in Spain?" he asked.

"I can," said Mickey with a smile. "There is music everywhere you go in Spain—and music is certainly a wonderful way to make friends."

Did You Know…?

There are many different customs and places that make each country special. Do you remember some of the things below from the story?

With its old buildings, churches, and palaces, Granada is one of Spain's most beautiful cities. Granada is well known for producing delicious chocolate and macaroni.

The Alhambra (al-HAHM-bruh) is a famous palace and fort in Granada. It was built long ago by the Moors, invaders from northern Africa who occupied southern Spain for centuries. In Arabic, the language spoken by the Moors, "Alhambra" means "red," the color of the fort's outer brick wall.

Raising sheep is a major industry in Spain. A lone shepherd may watch over hundreds of animals that graze on Spain's mountainsides and grassy plains.

Olive trees grow throughout Spain. Some of the trees are hundreds of years old. Instead of being grown for eating, most olives in Spain are harvested to make olive oil, which is used for cooking and in salad dressings.

Flamenco dancing was first performed by gypsies in southern Spain. It is an exciting dance form that is known for fast footwork, snapping castanets, and colorful costumes.

The guitar is the national instrument of Spain. Spanish guitars can be played solo, used to accompany folk singers, or featured in larger groups of musicians. The modern guitar was developed in Spain over a hundred years ago.

Most soups are meant to warm you up when it's cold outside, but gazpacho is meant to cool you off on a hot day. This spicy cold soup is filled with chunks of tomato, cucumber, and onion.

"Hasta luego" (AH-stah LWAY-goh) means "See you later," in Spanish.

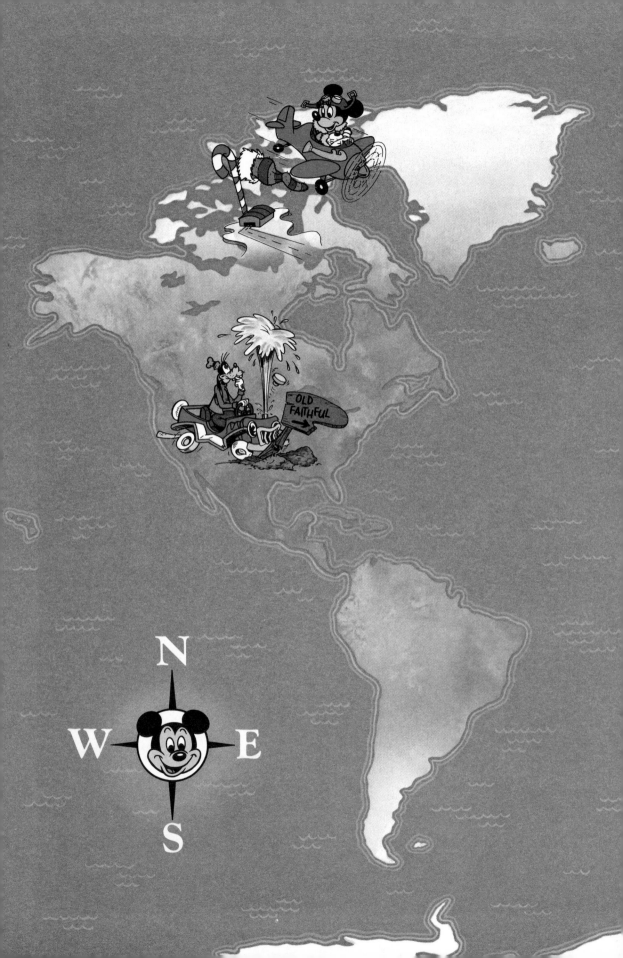